GH00865223

Fluffy Hugs

R. Dodd

Richard Dodd

Cover artwork and illustrations

Christopher Norman

DEDICATION

This book is dedicated to my wife and sons

For my best friend who provided the artwork
and inspiration for the story

Also to one Miss Devonshire (now Mrs
Tandy)…as promised so many years ago

CONTENTS

ACKNOWLEDGMENTS

This book was both a long time in the making and rushed out to meet a deadline. A dream a young boy had growing up reading many books by too many amazing authors to name. Thank you to all of them.
Main acknowledgments though to my very supportive family and Chris Norman - friend, artist and editor.

CHAPTER ONE

To look at Fluffy, you would think him ordinary. A normal, average little penguin. With his grey feathers and black eyes and beak, he is identical to every other little baby of his kind.

Fluffy *is* different however, not noticeable at first. Indeed, he hatched just the same as all the others. He was born in a zoo, but even this is not unusual. His parents are two of the biggest emperor penguins, so, it was a little surprising to the other penguins that Fluffy was so small when he was born. He was so cute and they were so proud, though, that they soon forgot about his small size.

Fluffy lived in an enclosure with his parents and twelve other penguins. Only three were emperor penguins. The enclosure was surrounded by glass so that the penguins could see the humans outside. There was a large pool of water for swimming and underground viewing so that they could see the people when they were underwater too. In one corner, there was a large hill made of snow. The penguins could walk to the top and slide down on their bellies into the soft snow below. Fluffy especially enjoyed the slide.

The little penguin quickly became a firm favourite within the zoo community. He was loved by his parents, obviously, adored by the other penguins, of course and the staff were understandably proud of the penguin born under their care. However, it was the visitors to the zoo whom Fluffy felt the strongest bond with. He loved watching them as much as they enjoyed looking at the new adorable baby penguin.

He knew how to make them happy and would dive head first down the icy slide, zooming past the cheering children viewing him happily, then he would waddle back along the ice, up the hill before sliding down on his belly back into the brilliant white of the powered snow. Yes, Fluffy loved his public and he really liked making them happy. He could almost sense their happiness through the glass and this made him extra happy.

The other penguins did not understand exactly why Fluffy cared so much for the humans and he did not know why no-one else felt the way he does.

"We are all animals, Dad." Fluffy said one day.

"We have wings and beaks and they have noses and legs, but we are all just animals, aren't we?"

"Yes son...I guess we are, but we are penguins and they are humans."

Fluffy knew better than to try to argue, as this was something they had spoken about lots of times before.

It was getting late in the day now and people were starting to leave the zoo. Fluffy shuffled up to the top of the hill for one last slide before sleeping.

There were not many humans left now, but one little boy had stopped to watch. He was a small boy, maybe four or five years old, wearing a rather large coat and a woolly hat. Winter had come around quickly this year. Fluffy was glad of this but the little boy was shivering. Fluffy looked at the boy from the top of his hill and saw the boy's brilliant blue eyes. He looked sad, perhaps because it was time to go home, but Fluffy sensed it was something more. He felt sorry for the boy and wished he could help him.

Instead of sliding down the slope into the snow, Fluffy turned and walked back down the hill and across the snow to where the little boy was stood watching.

A pane of glass separated the two youngsters, but for a second, it seemed to disappear.

Fluffy saw his chance, moving quickly (for a penguin) he hugged the little boy as well as he could. Ralph, for that was the boy's name, instantly felt happier and he closed his eyes enjoying his cuddle. When he opened them, the glass was back and Fluffy was right back on his side of it. Ralph smiled at his new friend and Fluffy appeared to smile right back at him. In that moment, Fluffy knew exactly what was wrong with the small child - he had been separated from his parents. Fluffy also knew that his parents would find him very soon.

Sure enough, even before the boy had turned around, he heard his mother calling to him. The boy waved to Fluffy and Fluffy raised a wing, wondering if he had just helped the human child or only imagined that he had.

CHAPTER TWO

With the general excitement of the zoo day, especially at feeding time, Fluffy had little time to think of his human friend in the days following. Although every time he saw a young child, boy or girl, he would recall the moment as if it had just happened that minute. He did not speak of it to either his mum or his dad.

One night, Fluffy could not sleep and his mind rolled over his experience with the young boy. The more he thought about it, the more convinced he became that it had actually happened. No way could it have been a dream he told himself. The question was then, how did someone (or something) make the glass disappear?

Fluffy felt that he simply had to attempt it again. He would test the theory and see if he could find the answer, like a police officer or a detective. That very night, he waited until all of the other penguins were fast asleep and crept slowly out towards the glass. There was no-one about, the zoo was silent. Darkness covered the world like a huge thick blanket. The moon was out but doing little to lighten up the night. There were very few stars.

Reaching the glass barrier, Fluffy paused. A few minutes went by and a few more. Nothing was happening, he could not understand it. Maybe he could only do it if a child needed help. Maybe he did not do it at all. Just as Fluffy felt hopeless, the glass shimmered and then disappeared completely.

Fluffy gulped and walked through the

space where the wall had been a few moments ago. He was outside the zoo. How exciting. How…scary! Quickly as he could, Fluffy waddled back inside the enclosure and sighed. That was quite enough excitement for one little penguin for one night.

CHAPTER THREE

Fluffy was happy. Until soon, he was surprised to learn that his parents were to be released into the wild. He had heard the zoo keepers talking. Of course, nobody believed that he could understand the humans. They couldn't, so why would Fluffy be any different?

"But Dad, I heard it…" Fluffy pleaded with his father to believe him. It was no good though. Fluffy began to learn that the more someone doesn't believe, the less you can talk to them.

"Listen son, sometimes you can imagine things that are not true or did not happen. That is alright as long as you are young. When you grow up, things will be different."

Fluffy did not believe that and he never wanted to grow up if it meant not believing someone he loved. He was happy with his parents but he felt that he was meant for more than just living in this enclosure. How he wished he could go to the wild with them. The zoo keepers thought he was big enough to be left without his parents but too small to go with them. He was frustrated but still did not want to be bigger!

The day quickly came when his parents were taken. The keepers wanted Fluffy to be asleep so as not to upset him. So, he went to a corner and pretended to sleep until they had gone with the humans. Fluffy was sad, but also excited. Today is the day I leave he thought to himself. I want to see a bit of the outside world and help some people. He decided to do this at night when it was dark. The other penguins were kind to him, but he knew they would not miss him too much. They would think that he went with his parents.

Fluffy spent the day practising his magic powers. He could make the glass disappear when he wanted now and reappear when he chose. He could also lift things up by thinking it. Not big things, but little things like snowballs, the bucket which the food came in and the cups which the humans drank out of on the other side of the glass.

He kept his magic a secret from the penguins and the humans. He had no clue why he could do these things. He wanted to use them to help though, he felt this was the reason he was magic.

As the sun went down and he thought more about leaving the zoo, the better he felt. Then, at about dinnertime, Fluffy could hear something. It was close, an animal in trouble, Fluffy could sense it. He had to go now. He thought hard and knew the staff were feeding the big cats at the moment and most of the humans were over that side of the zoo. He waddled over to the glass and it vanished before him. Fluffy walked through and set off, following the cries for help in his head.

He walked on and on. Past the monkeys, the zebras and the otters.

They were all fine. The noise was a cute little kangaroo with its foot stuck in a branch. The baby looked very cold and very sad. Fluffy walked through the fence, much to the kangaroo's surprise.

"Hello," he said, "my name is Fluffy. I am here to help you."

"Are you magic? My mummy says there is no such thing. But I knew that there was!" The little kangaroo smiled and forgot his foot for the moment.

"I think that I am magic" he said, sighing. "My parents didn't believe either."

The little kangaroo cried out again and Fluffy looked at his leg like a doctor would look at a poorly child. Fluffy was not sure how to help, so he trusted his feeling and gave the kangaroo a hug.

The branch moved away from the baby and his leg stopped hurting.

"Your mummy will be back soon" Fluffy

told the kangaroo.

The kangaroo hopped around and around. He was so happy. "Thank you Mr Fluffy!" He paused, a serious look on his little face. "Where will you go now?"

"I have work to do," said Fluffy. He turned and left the kangaroo hopping around his home.

CHAPTER FOUR

Fluffy soon learnt that he could travel to different places without walking if he just closed his eyes and thought about it. The first time it happened, he did not travel very far. He was thinking about the penguin enclosure and then, the next thing he knew, he was standing right by the glass.

Fluffy was very surprised. 'I really am very magical', he thought. Taking one last look at the twelve penguins, he heard another cry for help and, closing his eyes, he ended up appearing right next to the animal. It would have given the animal such a scare if the animal could see. The cry had come from a big ginger cat called Ringo who had got himself stuck in a carrier bag.

'What a strange name for a cat!' Fluffy thought to himself, unaware of the famous human drummer after whom the cat had been named.

"Hello?" He called. "Are you okay in there?"

"Of course I'm not" said the cat, crossly. "Those careless humans just throw rubbish anywhere."

"I am going to help you out of the bag" Fluffy said, feeling rather proud.

He could not see the cat's head as that was in the bag. He could only see Ringo's tail and one of his back legs. So, that is what he had to hug. It must have looked rather odd, a penguin hugging a cat's tail and one leg!

That is exactly what happened though and before long, the bag disappeared into a nearby bin and the big cat was free. He purred his thanks and began washing himself as if being trapped in a carrier bag had made him very dirty.

When he had finished his bath, the cat thanked Fluffy by sharing his fish supper which his humans had put out for him. The cat had lots of food in a very large bowl. He told Fluffy that it could probably feed five hundred, or maybe even five thousand little bellies. Fluffy did not understand, but he and Ringo ate a fish each and were nicely full.

Fluffy told Ringo of his magic while they ate. Ringo was not as surprised as Fluffy anticipated. He had seen magic before! Fluffy was pleased to learn that there were others like him but he was still eager to help everyone that he could. It was after he finished eating that Fluffy heard a call for help. It was a big call and sounded very far away.

"I have to go Ringo, someone needs help. It was very nice to meet you. Goodbye and thank you for the fish!"

The big cat meowed and rubbed against Fluffy to show his thanks. Then, Fluffy disappeared. The cry for help had indeed come from far away. France. Paris to be exact. Fluffy found himself looking up at the Eiffel Tower.

There was a small bird trying to keep away from a dog at the foot of tower. Fluffy had little time to rescue the bird as the dog was getting nearer and the bird did not seem to be able to fly away. Fluffy closed his eyes and used his magic to appear on the dog's back. There, he wrapped his little wings around the bulldog's neck and hugged him.

The dog stopped advancing toward the bird and instead asked,

"Are you okay little guy?"

"Y-y-yes thank you" Said the bird, more than a little surprised by this turn of events. "Except that I hurt my wing and I can't fly home."

Fluffy climbed down off the dog's back. "I can help with that" he said quietly. The little bird looked doubtful and rather fearful. Fluffy used magic again and hugged the bird before he could say another word. His wing was instantly better.

"How can I ever repay you?" He asked.

"Just be a good little bird" said Fluffy.

"I know that I will be good now" the dog said "and I shall maybe get Christmas presents this year!"

The little bird waved to his new friends and flew off back to his nest. The dog said his name is Spike and he high-fived Fluffy before going back to his home too.

CHAPTER FIVE

Christmas was getting closer and closer. The weather was getting colder and colder. Fluffy was loving the snow everywhere. He spent his days helping a few animals and listening to their stories. Sometimes they would share their food with him or find him somewhere to sleep.

He helped a deer, a racoon, a badger, a

mouse and a polar bear. Fluffy felt very happy to be helping so many creatures, but he was beginning to miss his parents. He would love to see them and be with them for Christmas but he had no idea how to find them. Instead, he worked hard listening to and answering calls for help. There were just three days left until Christmas now and Fluffy had been staying with his new polar bear friend for a couple of days, recovering and resting from all his heroics.

Now it was time to get back out into the world and help again. He answered a call which turned out to be from a little human girl. Fluffy used magic to appear next to the girl. She was so shocked that she fell over! When she stood up, she was covered in snow. She shook it all off and then asked,

"Are you here to help me? You are very cute and fluffy. I think you must be my angel or something"

Fluffy said, "That's my name!"

"What is? Angel?" she asked

"No Fluffy!" he said laughing.

"Wait, you can talk!" She gasped.

"Yes" he said, "How can I help?"

"It's my dad. He is stuck up there" she said, crying a little.

Fluffy turned and looked where she was pointing. Behind them on the edge of the cliff stood a huge lighthouse.

Fluffy gasped a little penguin gasp and looked up. He could not even see the top.

"The door is locked and can only be opened from the inside." The girl explained.

"I can take care of that" said Fluffy, now very confident of his ability.

The girl shouted "Come on then!" and ran off into the lighthouse.

Fluffy followed realising that she meant the door at the top was locked, not this one at the bottom. The girl, Susie, started on up the stairs. Fluffy stood at the bottom, trying to work out how to use the stairs without legs!

"I'll meet you up there" he called to her shutting his eyes tight and thinking of the very top of the tower. He appeared inside the room, looking out at the ocean. A man was on the floor, his wheelchair lay next to him. Fluffy shuffled over to the man. He had white hair and a big beard. He looked very happy and friendly despite his situation.

Fluffy told him that he would be okay. The old man smiled knowingly and spread his arms for the incoming cuddle. Fluffy reached down and hugged the man. As he did, the wheelchair disappeared and a bulging sack replaced its spot on the floor. The old man's tattered clothes turned into a bright red suit and when the door opened, the girl who walked in was not a girl at all. She was an elf.

CHAPTER SIX

Father Christmas stood up and put on his red hat with the white trim.

"Your turn to be surprised young Fluffy" he said kindly.

Fluffy was so surprised that he could not even talk! He had heard stories of Father Christmas both from the other penguins back at the zoo and on his travels.

He had never, ever expected to meet him.

"Sorry about tricking you Fluffy, but I knew you would come if you thought a child and an old man needed help." Father Christmas paused for breath. "It's your turn for some help now kiddo."

Still, Fluffy could not speak. He just stood and stared at Santa, beak wide open.

"We don't have much time" the elf said from by the door.

Fluffy found his voice, at last. "You are going to help me?"

"Of course," laughed Father Christmas.

"You have helped so many animals that it is about time you were helped. Let's go, I know where your parents are. They really want to see you."

Fluffy mumbled a thank you and hugged both Father Christmas and the elf.

The old man used his own magic and soon all three of them were riding in the sleigh towards the wild. Fluffy was very excited to see his parents. He looked down on the world and saw lights and water and trees. He could sense the happiness which was spreading ahead of Christmas.

Then he saw only whiteness.

Snow everywhere. The sleigh sped on,

faster and faster. There, ahead. Penguins. Thousands and thousands of emperor penguins. The sleigh stopped and Fluffy hugged Santa one last time. His parents came to the sleigh and Fluffy shouted with excitement.

"Mum, Dad, everyone! Merry Christmas!"

The End

Helping others brings its reward

FLUFFY HUGS

ABOUT THE PUBLISHER

Upbury Press was formed in 2015 with the sole purpose of bringing top quality children's books to the younger generation at an affordable, reasonable price. We pride ourselves on strong, original stories with a deeper meaning for children who learn from the characters whilst enjoying the story.

www.upburypress.co.uk

RICHARD DODD

ABOUT THE AUTHOR

Richard Dodd lives in Kent, with his wife and two sons. For as long as he can remember, he has written stories. At the tender age of ten, a teacher, Miss Devonshire of Luton Junior School told Richard that he could make it as an author and to dedicate his first book to her. Obviously those words stuck with him and he owes her a debt of thanks. Richard is in training to be a teacher himself now.

FLUFFY HUGS

ABOUT THE ARTIST

Christopher Norman also lives in Kent. He has always displayed a huge talent with any kind of artwork. Chris has a huge selection of outstanding paintings in his portfolio. Christopher also designs Christmas cards.

Cards can be bought at
www.rochestercards.co.uk

More information (and the original Fluffy) can be found at:

http://www.artgallery.co.uk/artist/chris_nor man

Fluffy returns with new adventures in Book 2 – entitled *Minty Visits*. Here is a sneak peek. Available now.

CHAPTER ONE

Now living in the wild, Fluffy is happy. A magical penguin is only ever truly happy when he is helping someone though. So, Fluffy is out a lot doing good deeds. His parents worried about him, but Father Christmas had assured them that Fluffy was a very responsible little penguin and would always be extra careful. It was strange for them having a magical son, when as far as they knew, they were not magic in the slightest. They were extremely proud however, particularly Fluffy's mother.

She had been heartbroken to leave Fluffy behind at the zoo. Knowing that there was nothing she could do did not prevent her from feeling guilty. She felt that she had abandoned her only son. When Fluffy had arrived on Santa's sleigh, she could not believe it. Fluffy was back! And he had met Santa! As she had listened to Fluffy's story, she came to realise that it was much better and much more complicated than she could have ever imagined. Her son was an international superstar.

Today, Fluffy was out on one of his missions. His parents and all of the other emperor penguins were eagerly awaiting his return. The babies were all babbling together, very excited and the adults...well, they were doing pretty much the same thing. They had all accepted that Fluffy was different and they celebrated him like royalty. There was no jealousy, simply adoration. He was one of them except that he had this magical gift. Everywhere that he went, Fluffy was admired and respected. He loved helping others and this really shone through. He had met many animals and people since he discovered his powers and now has many friends.

FLUFFY HUGS

Fluffy's best friend is Minty the polar bear. Even though they live at opposite ends of the world, they have lots in common. They are the same age and love to play together in the snow. Minty was wary of Fluffy's magic to begin with. It was just so different to anything he had seen before. Fluffy came by to help a little seal cub who was trapped. Minty saw him and they immediately struck up a wonderful friendship. They shared stories of their lives on the ice and Minty brought Fluffy home to meet his mum, dad and his brothers and sisters.

The polar bear family live in a huge cave in the side of an even bigger hill. They laughed when Fluffy asked if they had built it themselves. Apparently humans had made it and the bears had made it their own afterwards. Minty's mum offered to go out and fetch dinner, and that is when they all saw Fluffy's magic for the first time. Without giving any indication whatsoever, he closed his eyes and flapped his wings a little and suddenly a magnificent table appeared filled with bowls of fish. The polar bears were most surprised. A few of Minty's siblings clapped their paws together, but Minty just looked afraid.

"It's alright," said Fluffy, noticing his new friend was fearful, "I am a magic penguin and can make good things happen."

Praise for Fluffy Hugs:

By Lori A. Moore for Readers' Favourite

Fluffy Hugs, is a very cute and unique children's story. Fluffy Hugs would be the perfect book to read to little ones, either by a teacher in elementary school or at bedtime when a parent reads to a child. Children will like the "magic" part of Fluffy's ability to escape his enclosure and parents will like the message it sends to help others in need. Father Christmas even makes an appearance in Fluffy Hugs, Volume I, surprising Fluffy to reward him for all the good deeds he's done, but I won't spoil the ending by telling you what Father Christmas gives to Fluffy. Children will relate to the adorable penguin character.

Amazon Customer Reviews:

- Purchased for my 6 year old granddaughter we snuggled up together to read this beautiful tale of a magical penguin. Loving, caring full of kindness fluffy is inspirational to our younger generation. Looking forward to reading more. P. DAVIES

- The book was recommended to me so I bought it for my little grandson and he loves it. It's well written and illustrated.

- An enchanting children's story about Fluffy the Penguin would recommend

- An enchanting little story. I was drawn to the book by the really cute picture on the front...you can judge this book by its cover!

Lightning Source UK Ltd.
Milton Keynes UK
UKOW06f1605041116
286880UK00001B/4/P